·THE CHRONICLES OF·
NARNIA
THE LION, THE WITCH AND THE WARDROBE

THE CREATURES OF NARNIA

ADAPTED BY SCOUT DRIGGS

ILLUSTRATED BY JUSTIN SWEET

BASED ON THE SCREENPLAY BY ANN PEACOCK AND ANDREW ADAMSON
AND CHRISTOPHER MARKUS & STEPHEN MCFEELY

BASED ON THE BOOK BY C. S. LEWIS

DIRECTED BY ANDREW ADAMSON

HarperCollins *Children's Books*

WALT DISNEY PICTURES AND WALDEN MEDIA PRESENT "THE CHRONICLES OF NARNIA: THE LION, THE WITCH AND THE WARDROBE" BASED ON THE BOOK BY C.S. LEWIS
A MARK JOHNSON PRODUCTION AN ANDREW ADAMSON FILM MUSIC COMPOSED BY HARRY GREGSON-WILLIAMS COSTUME DESIGNER ISIS MUSSENDEN EDITED BY SIM EVAN-JONES PRODUCTION DESIGNER ROGER FORD
DIRECTOR OF PHOTOGRAPHY DONALD M. McALPINE, ASC, ACS CO-PRODUCER DOUGLAS GRESHAM EXECUTIVE PRODUCERS ANDREW ADAMSON PERRY MOORE
SCREENPLAY BY ANN PEACOCK AND ANDREW ADAMSON AND CHRISTOPHER MARKUS & STEPHEN McFEELY PRODUCED BY MARK JOHNSON PHILIP STEUER DIRECTED BY ANDREW ADAMSON
Distributed by BUENA VISTA PICTURES DISTRIBUTION THE CHRONICLES OF NARNIA, NARNIA, and all book titles, characters and locales original thereto are trademarks of C.S. Lewis Pte Ltd. and are used with permission. ©Disney Enterprises, Inc. and Walden Media, LLC. All rights reserved.

Narnia.com

The Lion, the Witch and the Wardrobe: The Creatures of Narnia

Book design by Rick Farley

1 3 5 7 9 10 8 6 4 2

ISBN: 0-00-720607-0

First published in the United States of America in 2005 by HarperKids Entertainment,
an imprint of HarperCollins Publishers, 1350 Avenue of the Americas, New York, NY 10019.

First published in Great Britain in 2005 by HarperCollins Children's Books,
an imprint of HarperCollins Publishers, 77-85 Fulham Palace Road, Hammersmith, London W6 8JB.

Printed in Italy.

One day, four siblings, Peter, Susan, Edmund and Lucy Pevensie, discovered a land full of magical creatures ruled by the White Witch, an evil sorceress. That land is called Narnia. Lots of curious and wonderful talking creatures live in Narnia. Some are good, but others are very, very bad. Come inside the wardrobe to meet them all!

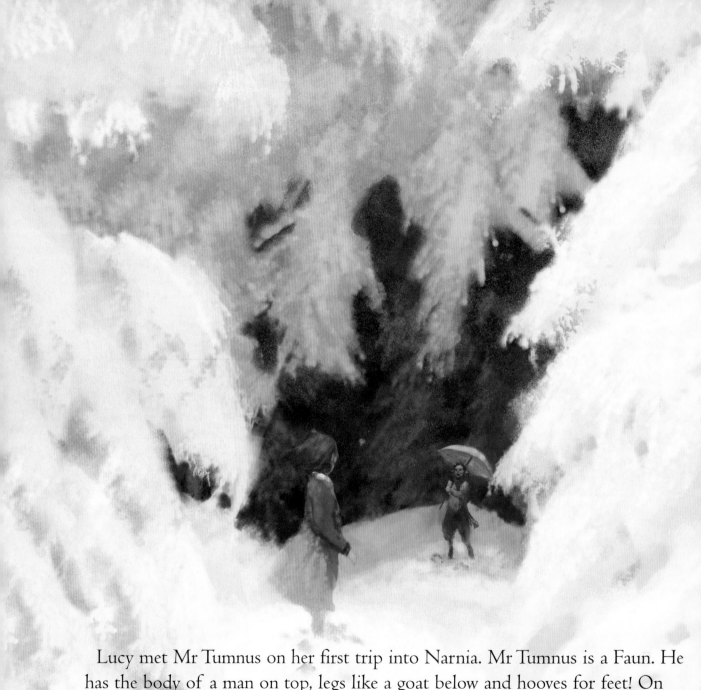

Lucy met Mr Tumnus on her first trip into Narnia. Mr Tumnus is a Faun. He has the body of a man on top, legs like a goat below and hooves for feet! On his head are two pointy horns.

Lucy had never seen a Faun before. But she was very glad that she met Mr Tumnus. He asked her to tea, and they got along so well that they were soon good friends.

Edmund didn't believe his sister Lucy when she told him about Mr Tumnus. He thought magical creatures were all imaginary. So he was quite surprised when he ran into a mean-looking Dwarf named Ginarrbrik.

Ginarrbrik is very small, not much taller than you. He has a long beard and wears a pointy hat. Some Dwarfs are good, but not Ginarrbrik. He is the driver of the White Witch's sleigh.

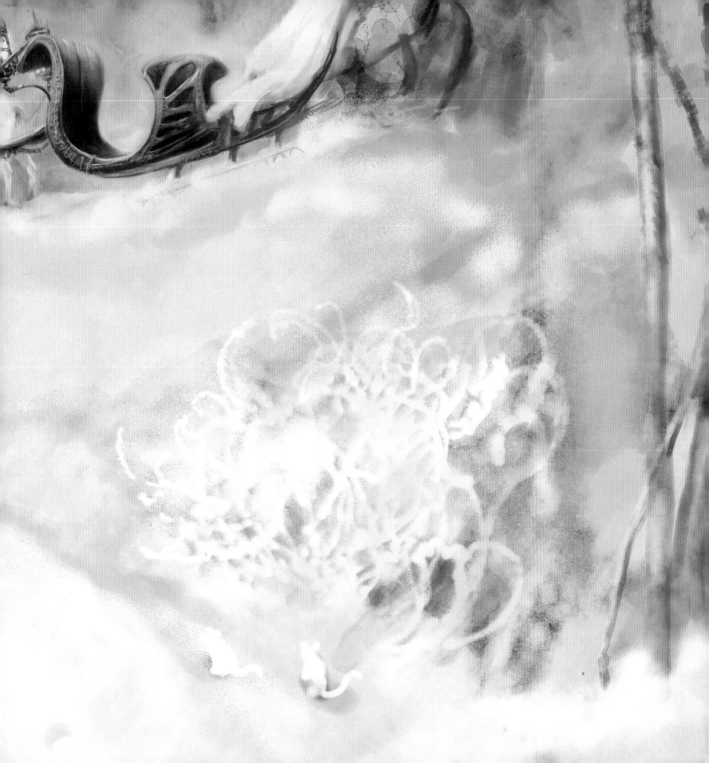

Edmund didn't realise it at first, but even though the White Witch looks like a great lady with fair skin and beautiful fur robes, she's not a lady at all. She's an enchantress who rules Narnia with dark magic.

More than one hundred years ago she cast a spell, making it always winter in Narnia. Even worse, with one quick flick of her wand, she turns innocent creatures to stone!

Not every creature in the forest is afraid of the White Witch. In fact, Mr
Beaver and many other noble creatures secretly plan to free their land from
her wicked curse.

When Peter, Susan, Edmund and Lucy met Mr Beaver in the forest, he
took them through the thick trees to his dam. Mrs Beaver prepared a
delicious meal, and Mr Beaver told stories about Narnia.

Mr Beaver started to tell the children about the White Witch and her terrible followers, but Edmund sneaked away while he was talking. Edmund should have listened to Mr Beaver, because at the Witch's castle he met Maugrim, the evil Wolf who is Captain of the Witch's Secret Police.

Maugrim uses his nose to follow
the White Witch's enemies through
forests and across mountains. He leads a
small army of Wolves who fight for the White
Witch. It is very hard to defeat the Wolves, but
sometimes they can be outsmarted.

Mr Fox is one of the cleverest animals in the forest. He isn't very large, but he makes up for it with his quick thinking.

When Maugrim and his Wolves were chasing Peter, Susan, Lucy and the Beavers, Mr Fox knew just what to do. While the children hid in a tree, he convinced the giant Wolf that they had already gone away.

Mr Fox and Mr Beaver could never defeat the White Witch on their own, even if all the creatures in the forest helped. But they had a very powerful friend.

They knew that Aslan, the true King of Narnia, would return. Aslan is a great and noble Lion. He will bring spring back to Narnia and free the land from the White Witch.

The children decided to go with the Beavers to join Aslan's army.
It was a dangerous journey, but they needed to save Narnia.

During their journey, they met a Dryad. A Dryad is a tree spirit that takes the form of a beautiful lady. The Dryad appeared out of a cherry tree that was blossoming for the first time in a hundred years!

Finally it was time for the great battle. The White Witch's army was a scary sight.

Cyclops, giant creatures with only one eye, marched around with huge clubs. Fearsome Minoboars wore spiky armour. Evil Harpies snarled their fangs and waved their long arms. And enormous Giants ripped up trees with their bare hands.

In Aslan's army,
the powerful Unicorn
reported for duty. Brave
Centaurs readied for battle.
Enormous Gryphons soared through
the sky. Fauns gathered their weapons.
Satyrs put on their shiny metal amour.

The battle was fierce, but with Peter, Susan, Edmund and Lucy's help, Aslan and his army brought peace back to Narnia.

Now it's time for you to go back to your world. Unless, of course, you would rather stay here. Do you think you'll be lucky enough to return to Narnia one day? One thing is certain — you will always remember its magical creatures.